The Discovery Books are prepared

under the educational supervision of

Mary C. Austin, Ed.D.

Reading Specialist and

Professor of Education

Western Reserve University

A DISCOVERY BOOK

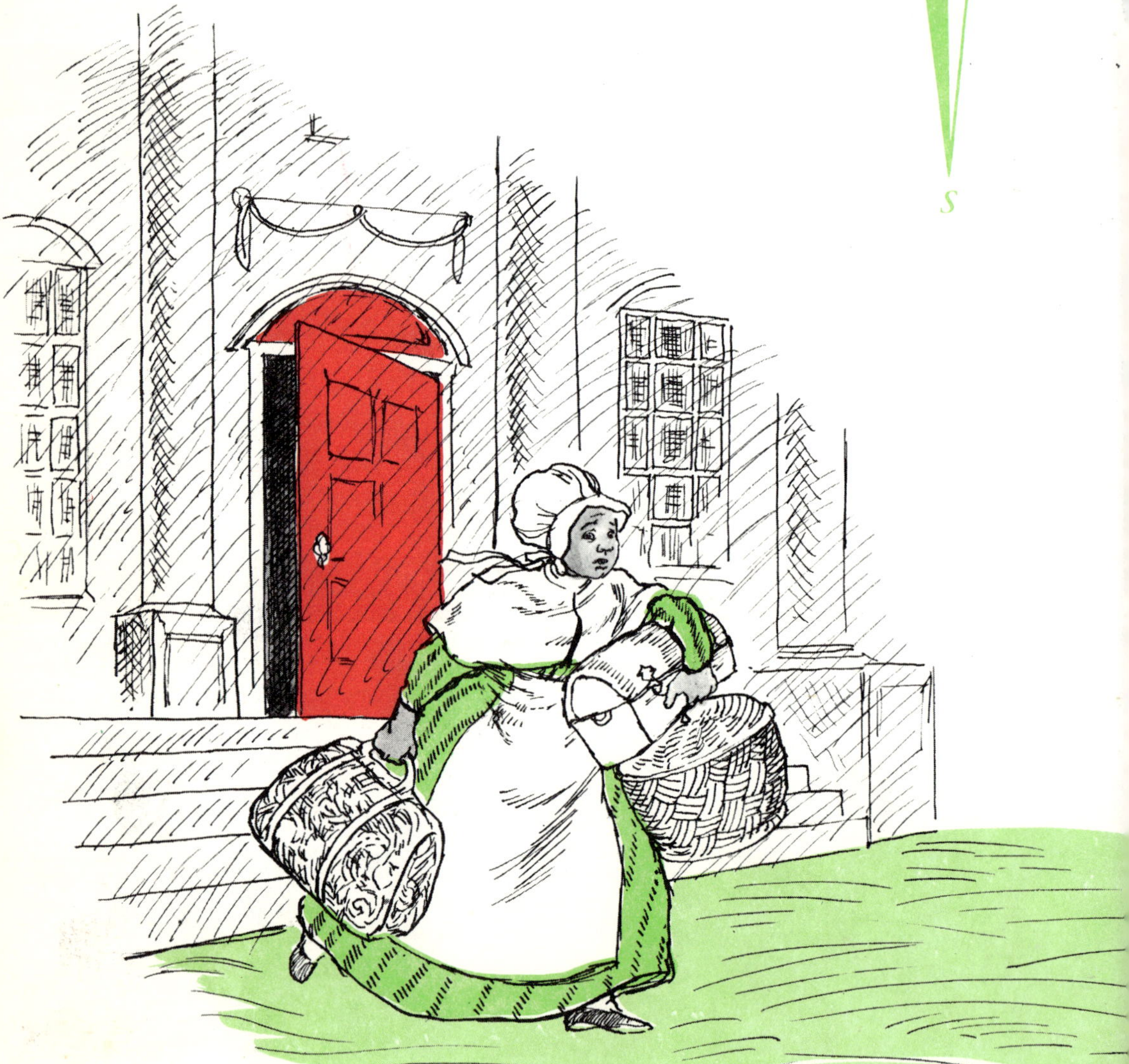

GARRARD PUBLISHING COMPANY
CHAMPAIGN, ILLINOIS

Dolly Madison

Famous First Lady

by Mary R. Davidson

illustrated by Erica Merkling

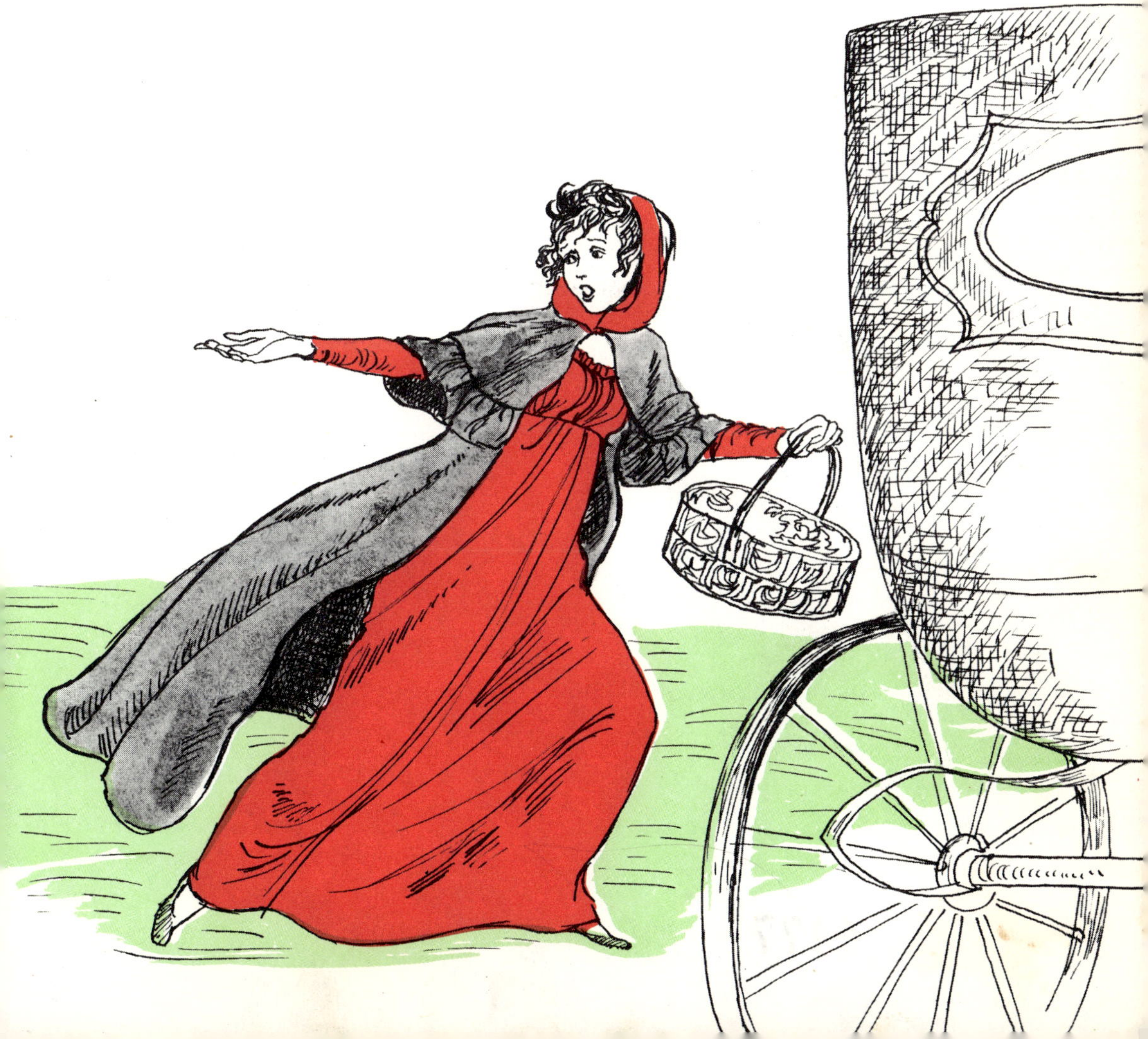

To Mary Richmond Oliver

Library of Congress Catalog Card Number: 66-13702

Contents

Dolly Madison: Famous First Lady

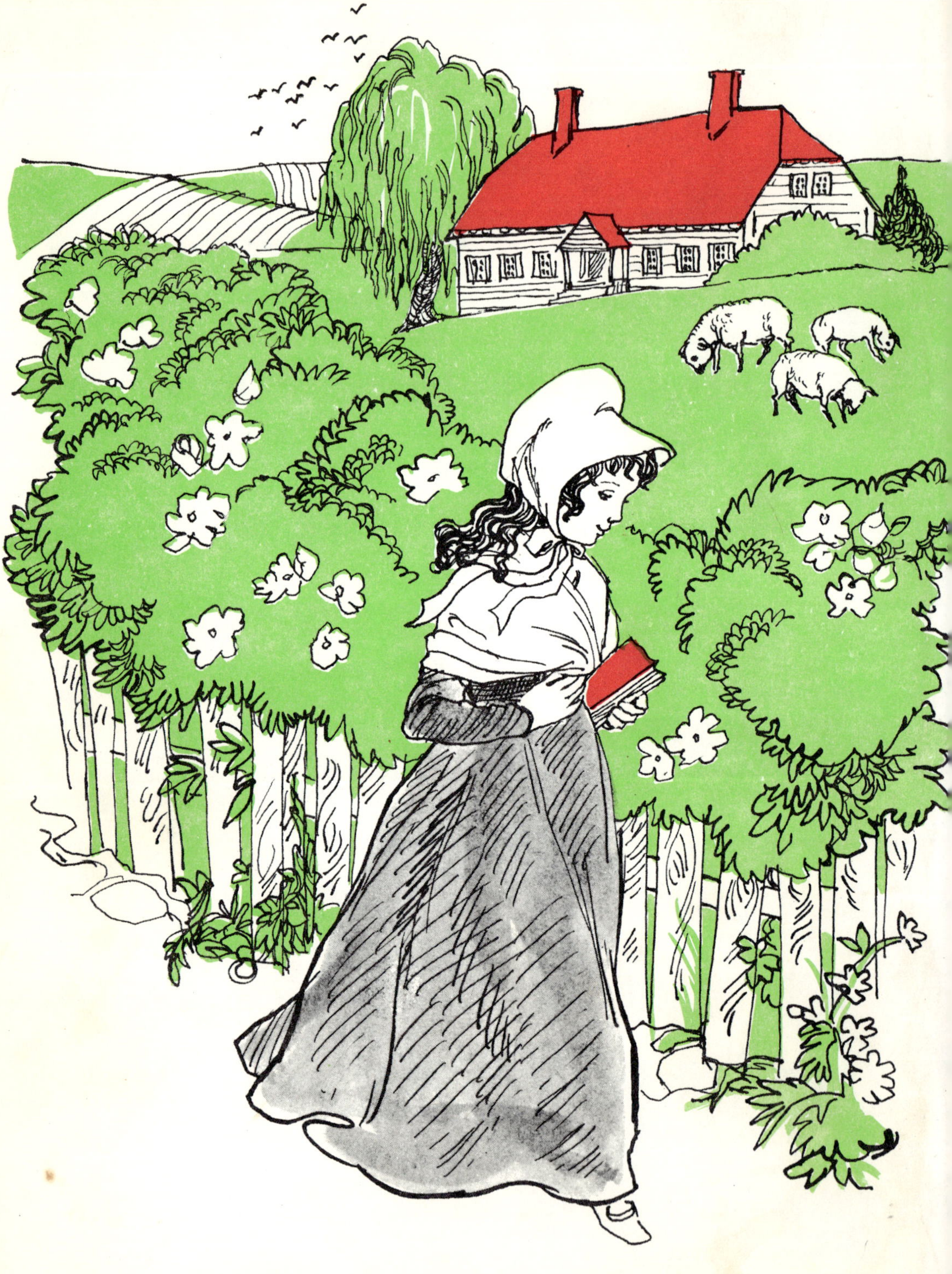

Chapter 1

The Little Quaker Girl

A little nine-year-old girl hurried along the path to school. Flowers bloomed all around her. Magnolia trees waved their white petals. Virginia was at its loveliest.

The little girl was Dolly Payne. She wore a simple gray dress that came down to her ankles. Around her neck was a white kerchief. Under this, on a string, hung her one treasure. It was a little gold pin that her grandmother had given her.

Dolly walked quickly into the schoolroom. She took off her sunbonnet and gloves. She felt under her kerchief to be sure that her pin was safe. She felt again. She couldn't find it!

"Dolly," the Quaker teacher said, "Thee is late. Take thy seat."

Dolly sat down. But her mind was on her pin. How could she have lost it! Somehow she got through school that day. She started home, looking carefully on both sides of the road. There was no pin.

She burst into the house, crying, "Mother Amy! Oh, Mother Amy!"

Mother Amy, her colored nurse, came hurrying. Dolly threw herself into her arms. "I've lost my pin," she sobbed. "I've looked everywhere."

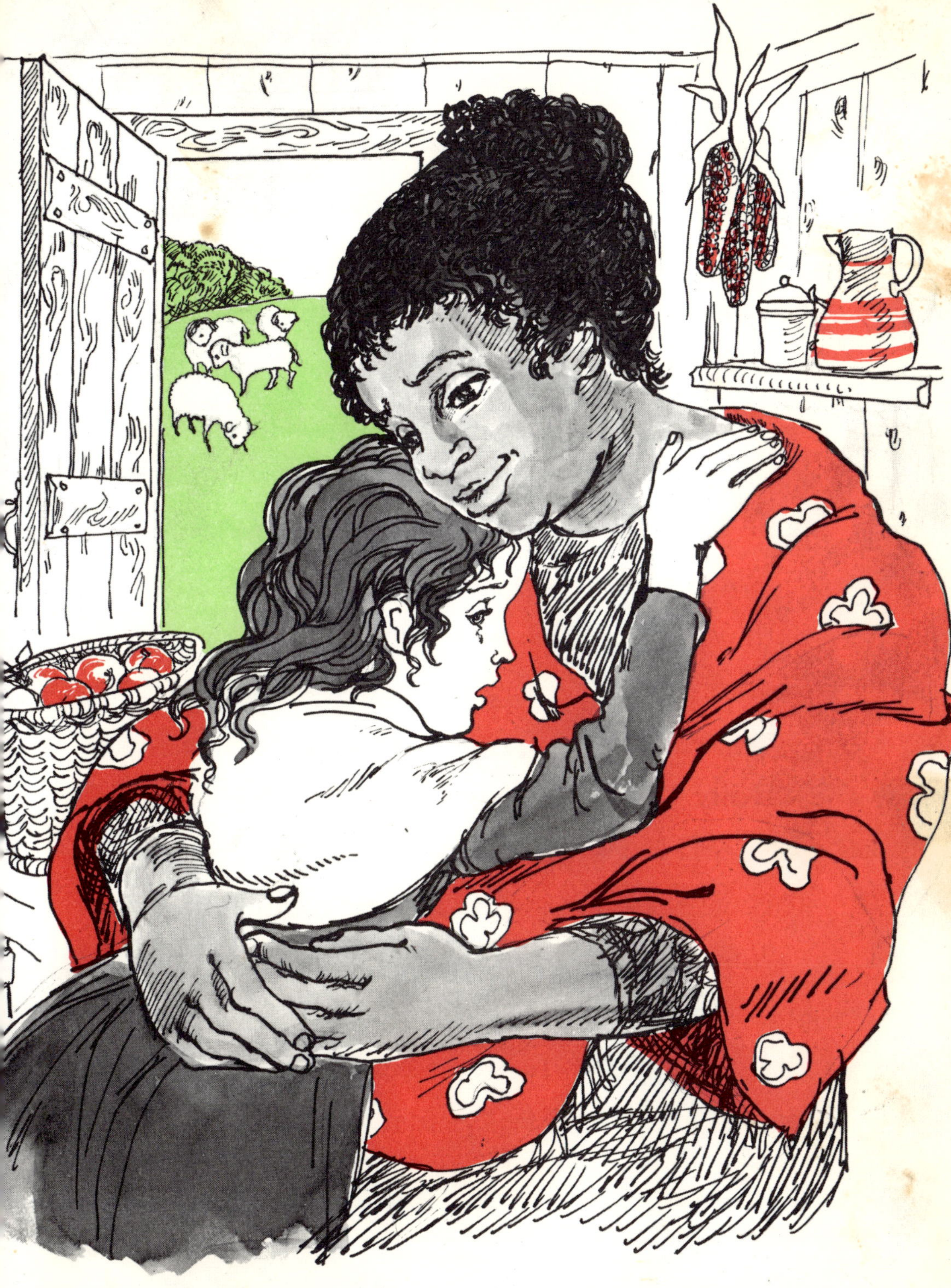

Mother Amy held her tight. "Your grandma will give you another," she said.

"If she did, I couldn't wear it, because we're Quakers," Dolly sobbed.

Mother Amy spoke more firmly. "Some day, I tell you, you will have lots of gold pins and necklaces. You'll have silk dresses, and velvet ones too."

Dolly looked up, her blue eyes bright with tears. "Do you *really* think so, Mother Amy?"

"I really do. You just wait, honey."

Dolly (sometimes spelled *Dolley*) was born in North Carolina in 1768. Soon afterwards, her parents moved to Virginia.

The Paynes had two sons, Walter and William Temple, who were older than Dolly. There were five younger children: Isaac, Lucy, Mary, Anna, and Johnny.

Dolly and Lucy were always close friends. And Dolly loved little Anna dearly.

Dolly's parents were Quakers. Like most Quakers, Mr. Payne hated fighting. During the Revolutionary War he stayed quietly on his farm, working his fields and feeding his cattle. He did not believe in slavery, for he felt that all men are brothers. He wanted to free the slaves who helped him on his farm, but the laws of Virginia would not allow him to. Mr. Payne helped the poor and cared for the sick. He dressed always in plain Quaker gray.

Dolly's father had not been a Quaker all his life. He had become one when he married Dolly's mother. It was his mother, Mrs. Payne, who had given Dolly the little gold pin.

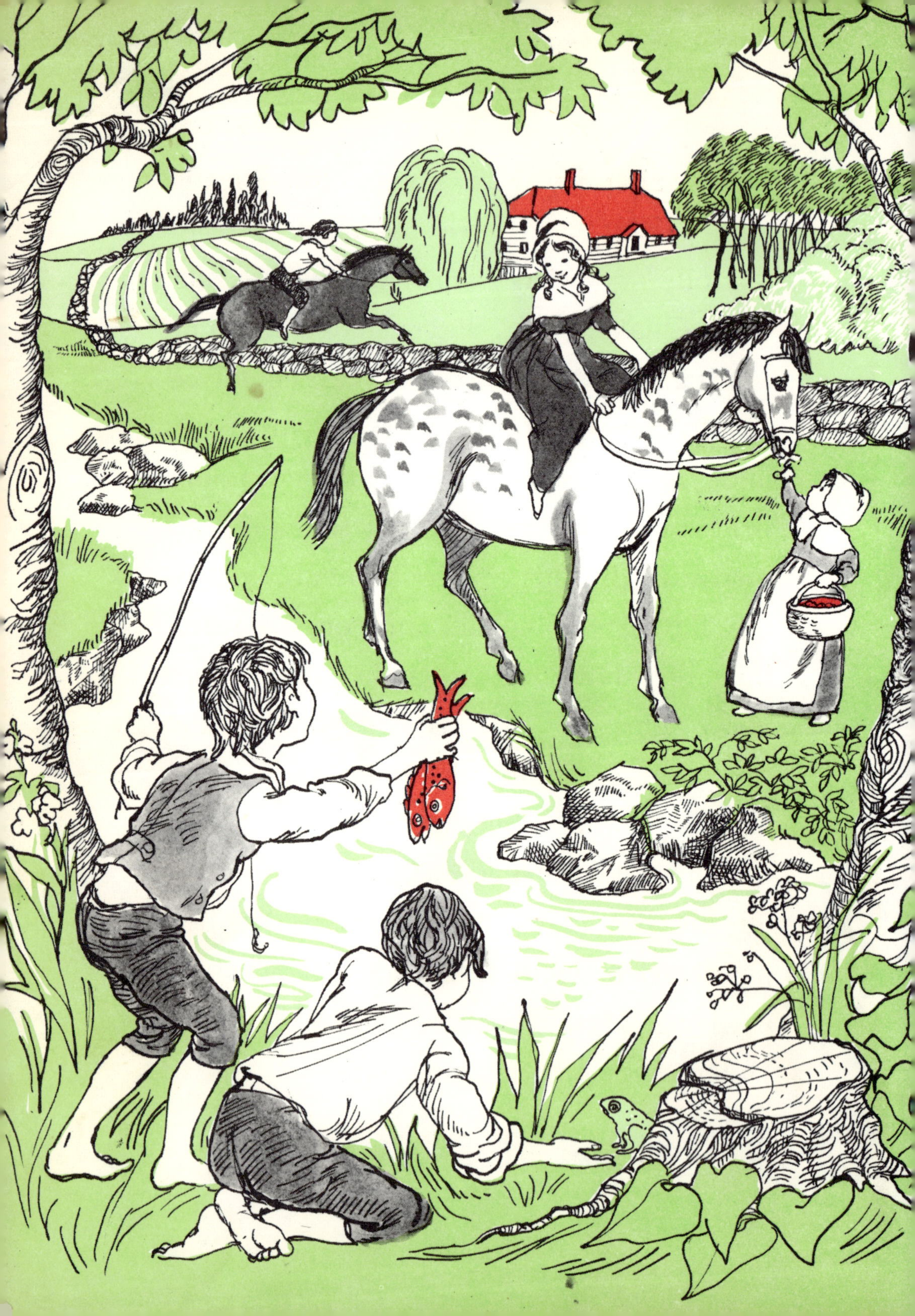

When Dolly was seven, the Paynes moved to Scotchtown. It was a larger plantation. They had a big house with nineteen rooms. Green fields were all around. A brook, where the children fished, ran through the fields. Every day the children rode horseback, jumping the brook and the stone walls.

The older children attended the nearby Quaker school. There they learned reading, writing, and some arithmetic. Dolly wrote beautifully, but she spelled as she pleased. She spelled *uncle,* "unkle" and *writing,* "wrighting."

Dolly learned as much at home as she did at school. Mrs. Payne was an excellent cook and a woman of great energy and charm. She taught Dolly how to sew, cook, and nurse the sick.

When Dolly was twelve, she made a "trifle." She baked three layers of sponge cake in the brick oven. While these were still hot, she brushed them with rum. Then she spread raspberry jam between the layers and sprinkled sugar on top.

At supper that night, Mr. Payne said, "Mother, this is the best trifle you ever made."

"Your eldest daughter made it," she said. "She'll be a fine cook some day."

After supper the whole family gathered in the living, or "keeping," room. There, standing before the open fire, Mr. Payne read to them stories from the Old Testament. The children listened eagerly.

After this they said good-night. Each one took a candle and went up to bed.

Chapter 2

Philadelphia

One day when Dolly was fourteen, Mr. Payne called the family and servants together.

"Children," he said, "we are going to move."

There was silence.

Mr. Payne went on. "Virginia has changed the law about freeing slaves, so at last I can free ours. But I will not be able to run the farm without them. We are moving to Philadelphia where I will go into business."

"Don't free *me,* Mr. Payne," said Mother Amy. "I want to stay and take care of my children."

Mr. Payne smiled. "I'll have to free you, Mother Amy," he said. "But you may stay with us. I'll pay you wages."

It took a year to free the slaves and sell the plantation. At last the Paynes packed up their baggage and started for Philadelphia.

Philadelphia was the largest city in the nation. After the quiet of Scotchtown, it seemed crowded and noisy.

But the Paynes' house seemed very small. Mr. Payne needed the big room downstairs for his new business of starch-making. Upstairs there were only six rooms. Dolly had to share a bedroom with her three sisters.

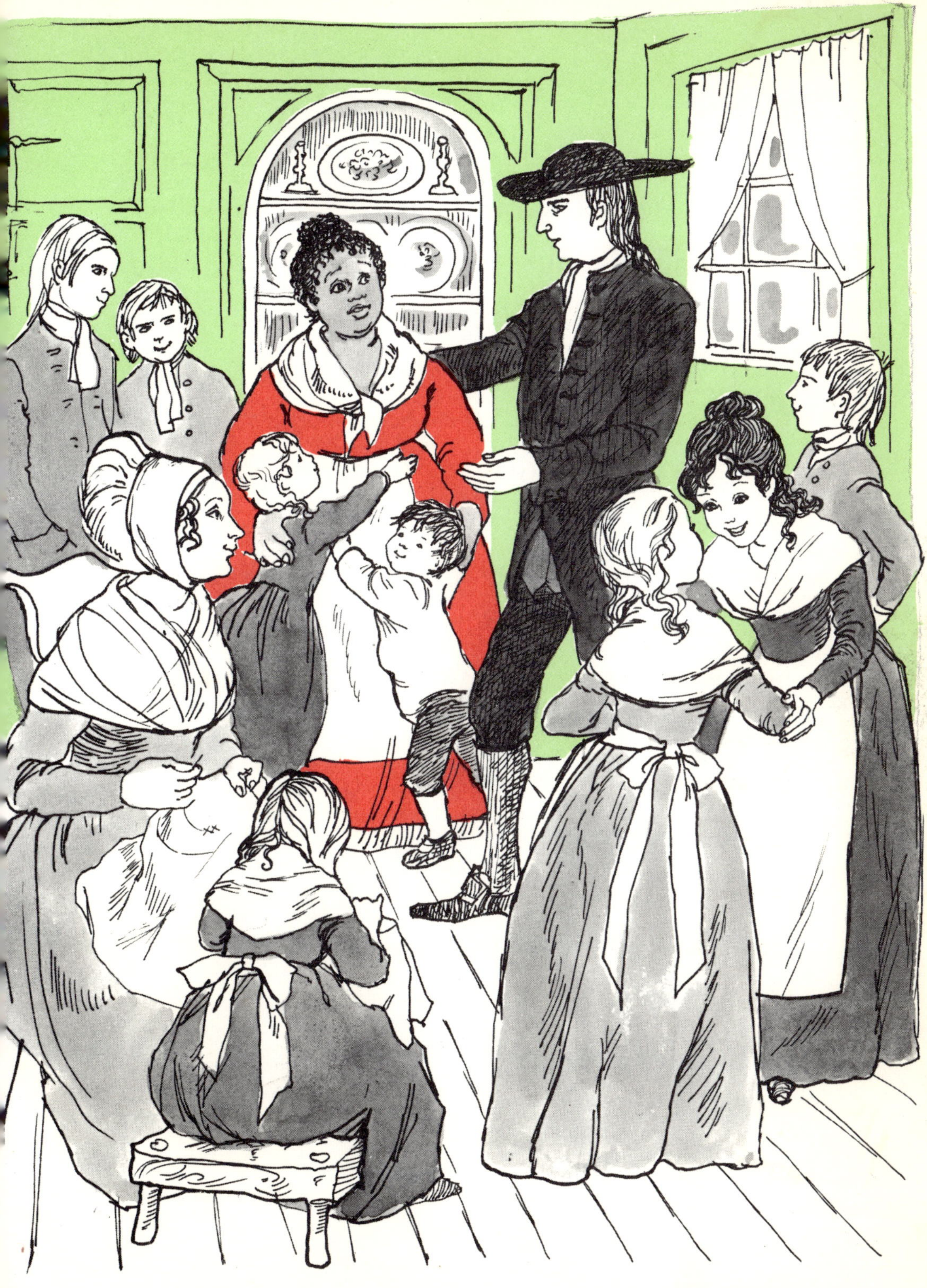

The younger children went to school. Dolly's school days were over, but she had classes in religion. These, her father felt, were important.

In the morning, Dolly helped her mother cook. In the afternoon, she took long walks with Sally Drinker, her Quaker friend. Their favorite walk took them through the shopping district. Here the stores were filled with beautiful gowns and hats. Some had come straight from Paris. Dolly and Sally both wore plain gray Quaker dresses, but how they longed for beautiful clothes! One day some new styles were shown.

"Oh, Dolly," Sally cried, "look at that yellow velvet gown! How I'd like to have a dress like that!"

They looked in the next store window.

"Look at those little French dolls!" Dolly cried. "They're adorable! Oh, Sally, let's come here often!"

Dolly had a chance to meet other people, too. When she was eighteen, she was invited to visit Quaker friends who had a tavern on the King's Highway. Great coaches drawn by four horses stopped there, on their way to New York. Dolly often ran out to greet the passengers. And so she came to know many people who were not Quakers.

The following year the Constitutional Convention was held in Philadelphia. Famous statesmen from all over the country were there, planning the new government. At any time Dolly might see George Washington or Benjamin Franklin walking down the street.

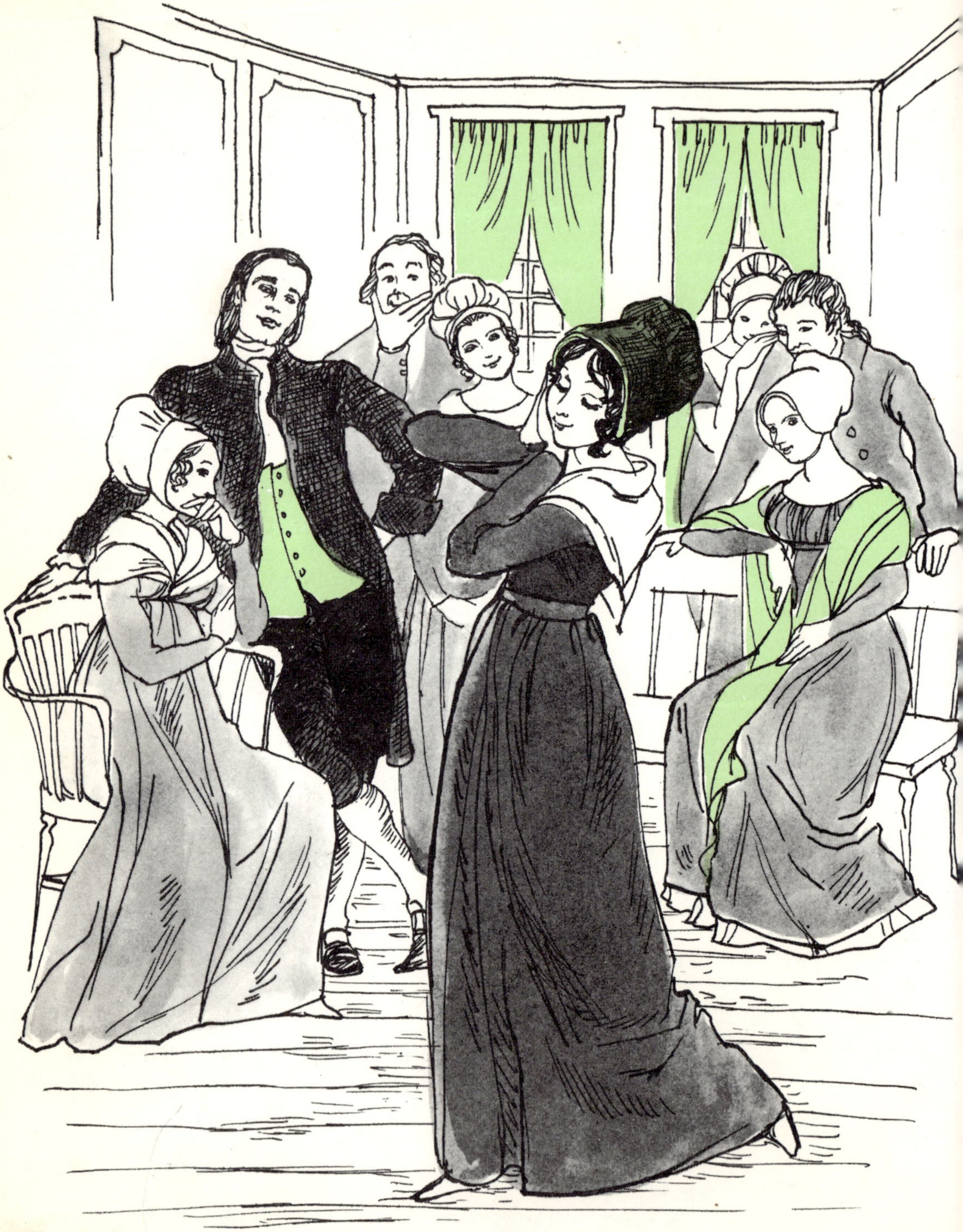

Chapter 3

Marriage to John Todd

In Philadelphia Dolly was invited to all the parties for young Quakers. No dancing or card playing was allowed. Instead the guests played charades or forfeits.

Many young men admired Dolly. But one young man usually took her home from parties and Quaker meetings. His name was John Todd. John was a young law student. He spent more and more time with Dolly and came to love her.

One night, after John had known Dolly three years, he stopped with her outside her door. He was silent a moment. Then he said, "Dolly, you and I have been together often. You must know that I love you. Will you marry me?"

Dolly hesitated.

John pleaded, "We are both Quakers, and we have the same friends. I think I can make you happy."

Still, Dolly was silent. Then she said, "Oh, John, I don't want to be married yet, not to anyone. Perhaps someday . . ."

"Then I'll wait," said John. "But I'll always be here to help you and your family. And I'll continue to hope that someday you will say yes."

He bowed and left.

Afterwards Dolly kept thinking about John. She *did* like him. But in her heart she hoped sometime to get away from the narrow Quaker life. She wanted to meet all kinds of people, to be like other girls.

Meanwhile her father was steadily losing money. Mr. Payne had been a good farmer, but he was a poor business-man. Finally the time came when he could not pay his bills. This made him so discouraged and unhappy that he became sick.

One night he called Dolly to his room. She went to his bedside and gently took his hand.

"Daughter," he said feebly, "has John Todd asked you to marry him?"

Dolly nodded. "Yes, Father," she said.

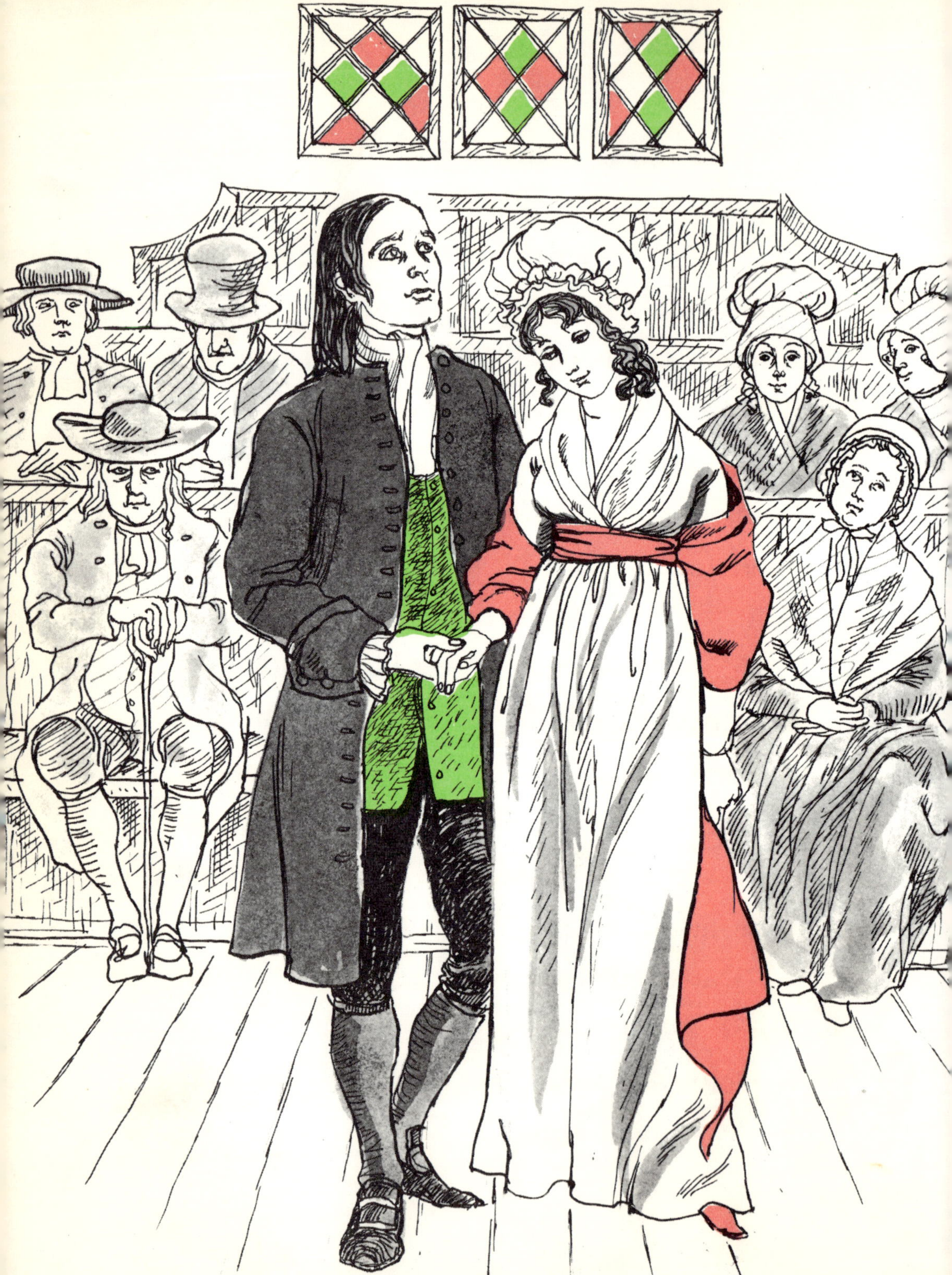

"Do you like him?"

"Oh, yes, Father."

"Dolly, John would always love and take care of you." He paused. "I want you to marry him, daughter."

Dolly had always obeyed her father. Now, as she looked at him, lying weak and sick, she suddenly grew up.

"I will, Father," she said. "I'll tell him tonight."

A short time afterwards, Dolly Payne and John Todd were married at the Quaker meetinghouse. They promised "in the presence of God and of these witnesses" to love each other and "be faithful unto death."

Eighty people had been invited to the wedding. Afterwards they all went to the Paynes' house for a wedding supper.

John was now a successful lawyer. He bought Dolly a house on Chestnut Street in Philadelphia. Later he bought a larger house with a stable and a carriage. For the first time in her life Dolly could have beautiful things. She bought fine mahogany furniture, curtains, silver, and glass. She loved to keep her house shining and bright.

After two years Dolly and John had a little son. They named him Payne, for Dolly's father.

Dolly was truly happy now. She had a lovely home, a baby boy, and a loving husband.

Chapter 4

The Yellow Fever

Soon after Dolly's son was born, Mr. Payne died. Dolly's mother had to find a way to support herself.

Philadelphia was now the capital of the United States. There were many congressmen looking for places to take meals. As Mrs. Payne was famous for her cooking, she started a boarding-house. The young congressmen liked her home-cooked food better than the meals at The Indian Queen, Philadelphia's one hotel.

Lucy, Mary, and Anna lived with their mother and helped her run the boardinghouse.

Dolly came to see her mother often. She enjoyed meeting the congressmen and talking about the government. Aaron Burr, a senator from New York, became a special friend.

One day there was great excitement at Mrs. Payne's boardinghouse. Lucy Payne, aged fifteen, had suddenly eloped with George Steptoe Washington, the President's nephew. Lucy went to live at Harewood, George's home in Virginia. Later she invited her mother and Mary to live with her.

The Paynes were disappointed that Lucy had not married a Quaker. But the marriage proved to be a happy one.

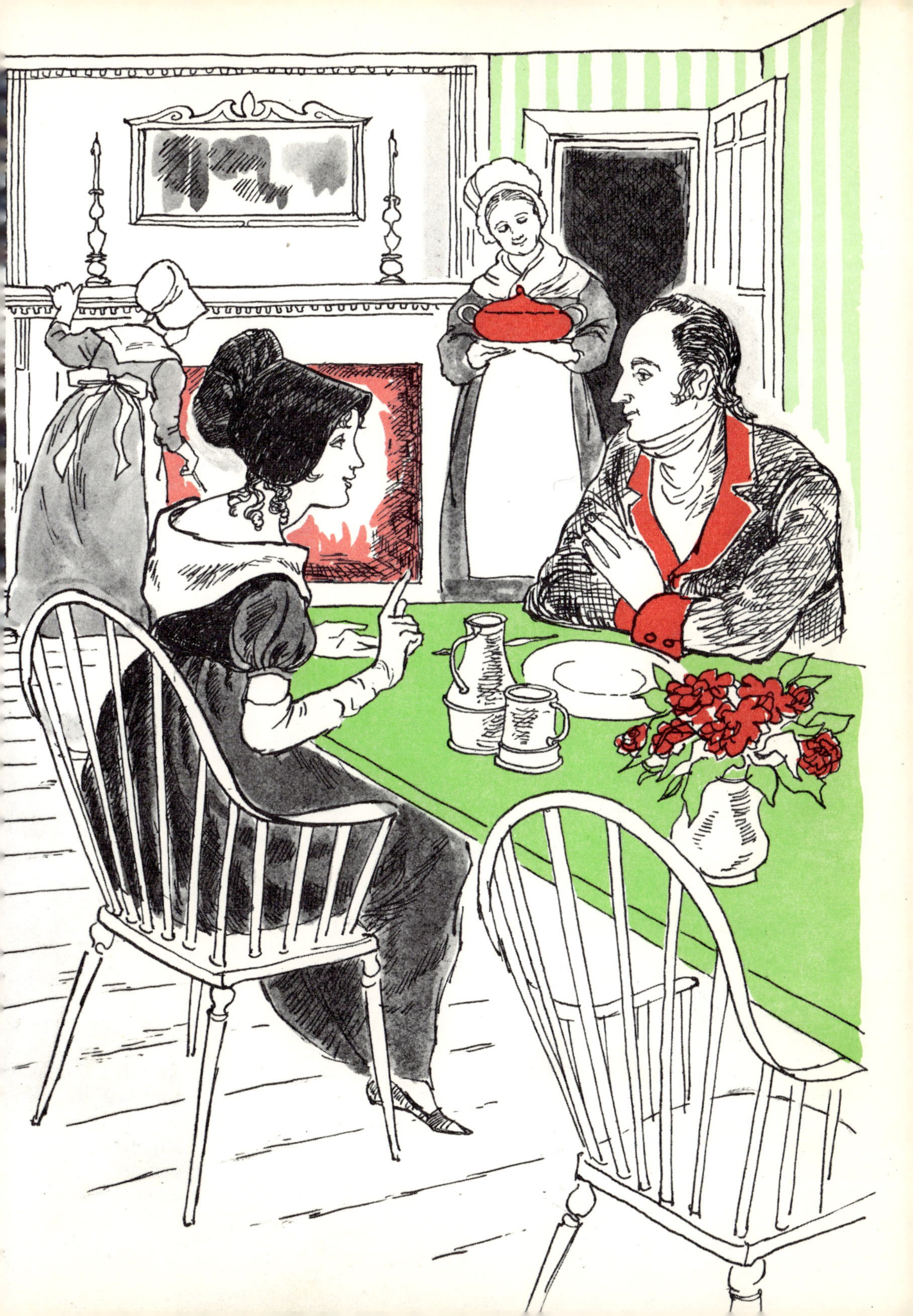

Dolly and John now had another baby, a boy named William. They were happier than ever. But suddenly, a dreadful sickness that people called the yellow fever swept Philadelphia.

No one was safe. The fever victims suffered terribly. They died in a few hours. The doctors didn't know what to do. They drew blood from people. They fired cannons, hoping to clear the air of fever. Nothing could stop the epidemic. Everyone tried to get out of the city.

John Todd took Dolly and the children to a safe place in the country. Then he hurried back to Philadelphia. John gave money to help the sufferers. And, like a good Quaker, he himself took care of the sick and dying.

Then his parents, who were still in the city, came down with the yellow fever. John wrote Dolly that he was looking after them.

Dolly was terribly worried. She knew John was very tired. She was afraid he would be sick himself.

In spite of everything John did, his parents died. He attended to the burial. Then, on horseback, he started for the country and Dolly.

As he was riding, he began to have dreadful pain. He knew what that meant, for he had taken care of many people with the yellow fever. His one thought was to see Dolly again. As he rode, he kept saying over and over again, "I must see *her*! I must see *her*! I must see *her*!"

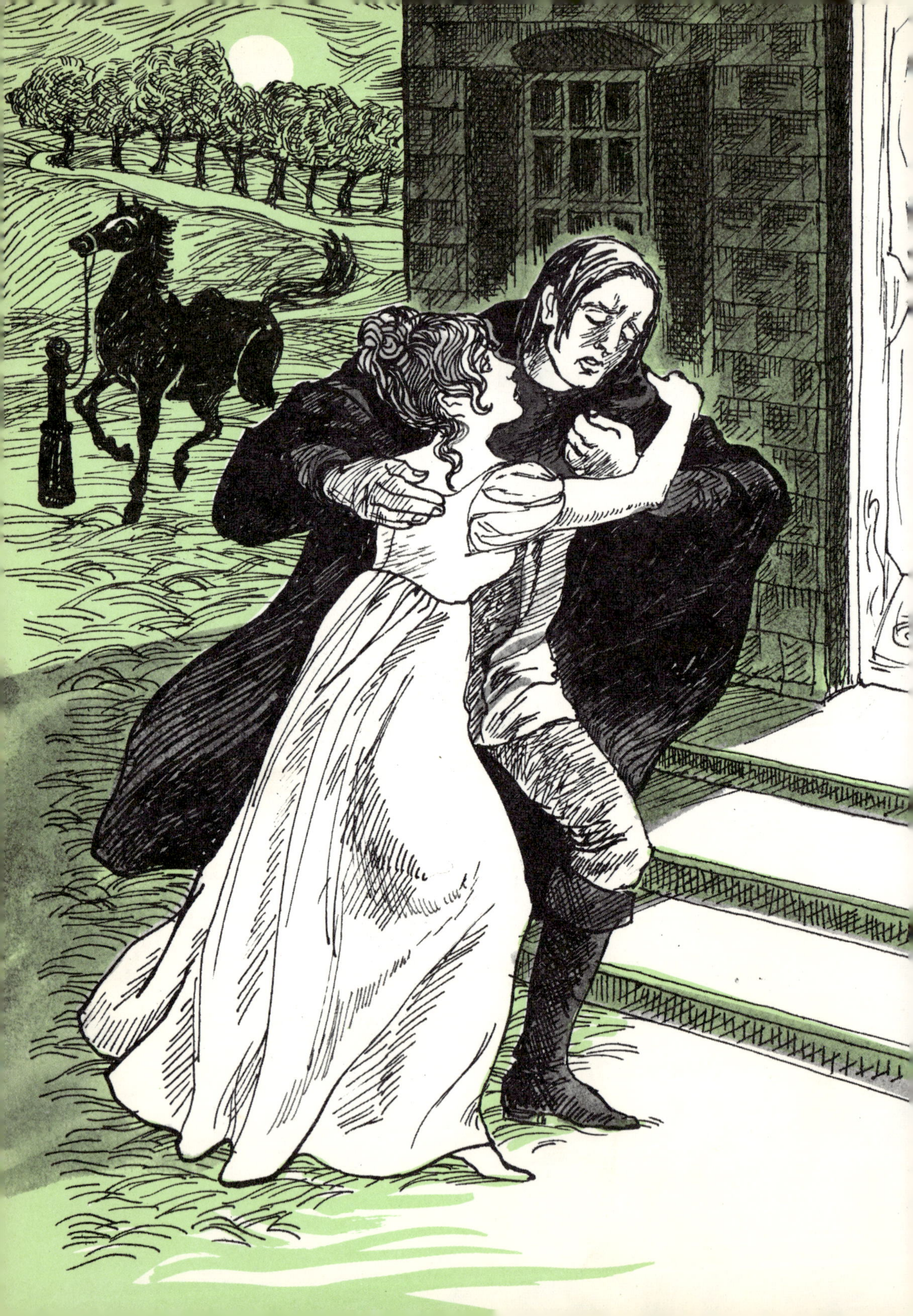

So he kept on going. He did reach Dolly. She ran out to meet him. She knew he was sick, but she was not afraid. She threw her arms around him. She helped him from his horse.

"John, dear," she whispered.

But John could not answer her. He died almost immediately.

The very next day, Dolly herself was sick. Her mother came at once to nurse her. Dolly fought her way through the fever. She began to get well. Bravely, she tried to face the idea of life without John.

Then one morning Mrs. Payne came into Dolly's room. Her face was very sad.

"Dolly," she began, "the baby . . ."

"Not the yellow fever!" Dolly cried.

"Oh, Mother, not the yellow fever."

Mrs. Payne nodded. "I'm afraid it is," she said softly.

"Please bring him to me, Mother."

Mrs. Payne brought in the three-month-old baby. Dolly looked at him. She knew that nothing could be done. The little boy lived only a few hours. Dolly held him to the end.

This was the hardest time in Dolly's life.

Chapter 5

Mrs. James Madison

When Dolly returned to Philadelphia, her sister Anna came to live with her. Dolly got well surprisingly fast. As she grew stronger, she became prettier than ever. People turned to look at her on the street.

Her friend, Aaron Burr, came to call often. One day Burr said to Dolly, "James Madison would like very much to meet you. May I bring him over some afternoon?"

Dolly said, "Of course!"

Madison was a congressman from Virginia. He was a famous man who had done much of the planning of the Constitution. And then, with Alexander Hamilton and John Jay, he had written the *Federalist Papers.* These papers were written to get people to approve the Constitution. Madison had kept a record of the debates at the Constitutional Convention. This record was valuable because it was the only one.

Now Madison was working on the famous amendments to the Constitution which were later called the Bill of Rights.

Madison was brilliant and wealthy, but he was rather quiet and shy. He was seventeen years older than Dolly.

Burr took him to see Dolly as planned.

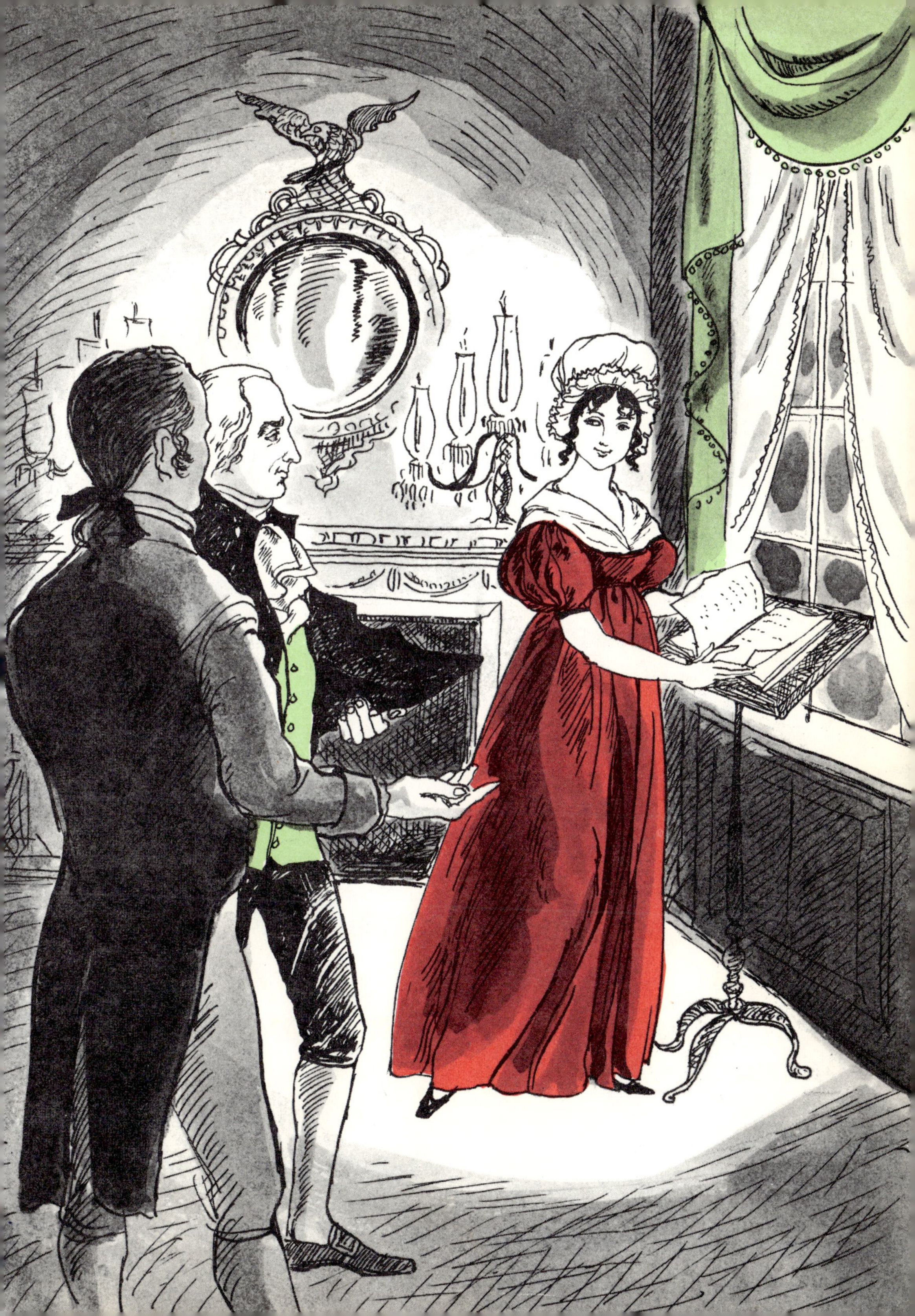

They found her in a room lighted by many candles. She wore a dark red satin dress with a fine white kerchief. A little lace cap was on her dark curls. Madison had never seen anyone so lovely. That afternoon he fell in love with her.

Madison wanted to be married at once, but Dolly hesitated. She wanted to have time to think things over, so she went to visit Lucy in Virginia. On the way she stopped at an inn. Suddenly she knew she wanted to marry Madison.

Madison hurried to Harewood, Lucy's home. He and Dolly were married there.

Dolly's first wedding had been a quiet one. But this wedding was very gay. There was dancing. Violins and banjos played minuets and reels.

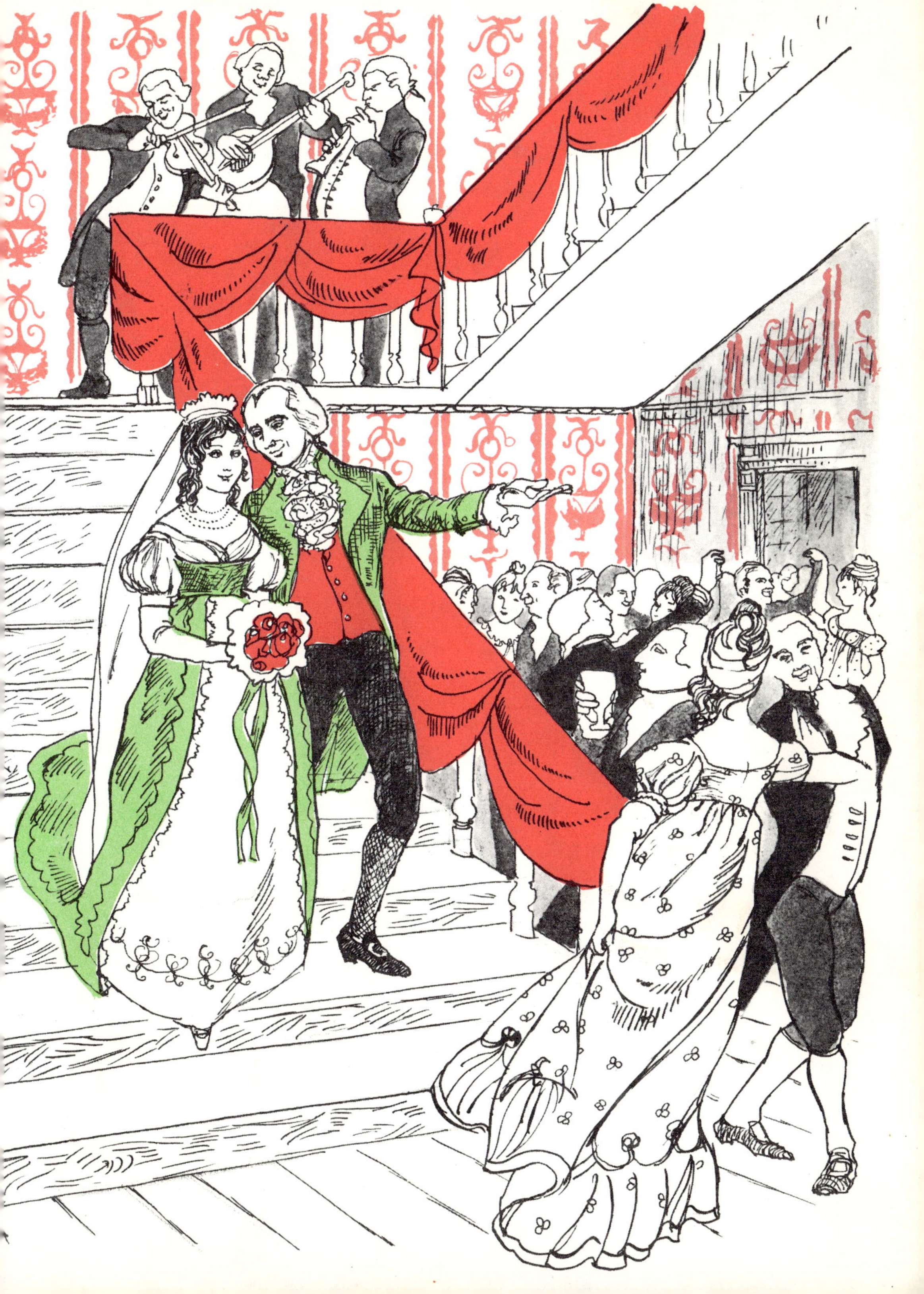

"Ladies change. Grand right and left," the caller shouted.

Dolly wore a beautiful wedding gown. Madison wore a silk coat, and he had diamond buckles on his shoes. Ladies cut off pieces from his ruffled shirt to keep as souvenirs.

Finally Dolly and Madison got away in a shower of rice and flowers.

Madison had wanted to take Dolly to Montpelier, his home in Virginia. But there was no time for a honeymoon. He was needed in Philadelphia.

Madison was not a Quaker, and Dolly herself was no longer a Quaker. She now wore the gay dresses and jewelry that she had longed for as a girl. But she never forgot the Quaker lessons of duty and kindness.

Her first thought was always for her husband. As Madison was not strong, it was necessary to guard his health.

Payne, too, was always on her mind. But she was not wise with him. She let him do anything he wanted. Madison, who loved Payne as if he were his own son, also spoiled him.

Dolly enjoyed being with her sisters. Anna still lived with her. Mary was invited up from Harewood. The three sisters went to parties and balls. Dolly wanted them to have all the fun that she herself had missed as a girl.

Dolly had never learned to dance. But Anna and Mary had learned how. They had many a gay time with their older sister as chaperone.

Chapter 6

The Nation's Hostess

When Dolly married Madison, there were two political parties in America. There were the Federalists and the Democrats. The Federalists believed that the rich landowners and businessmen should run the country. The Democrats thought that the common people should have more power. In 1794 John Adams, a Federalist, became President. Madison, a Democrat, left Congress and went home to Montpelier.

Madison's estate was at its loveliest. The brick house stood high on a hill facing the Blue Ridge Mountains. Someone said that Montpelier was only "a squirrel's throw from heaven."

Dolly loved Montpelier. She loved the flowering trees, the redbud, and dogwood. She liked to work in her garden.

Shortly after his marriage, James added a portico and wings to the square house. His mother and father moved into the south wing.

Madison kept in close touch with politics. He and Jefferson, then Vice-President, wrote to each other often.

In 1801 Jefferson himself was elected President. The first thing he did was to make James Madison his Secretary of State.

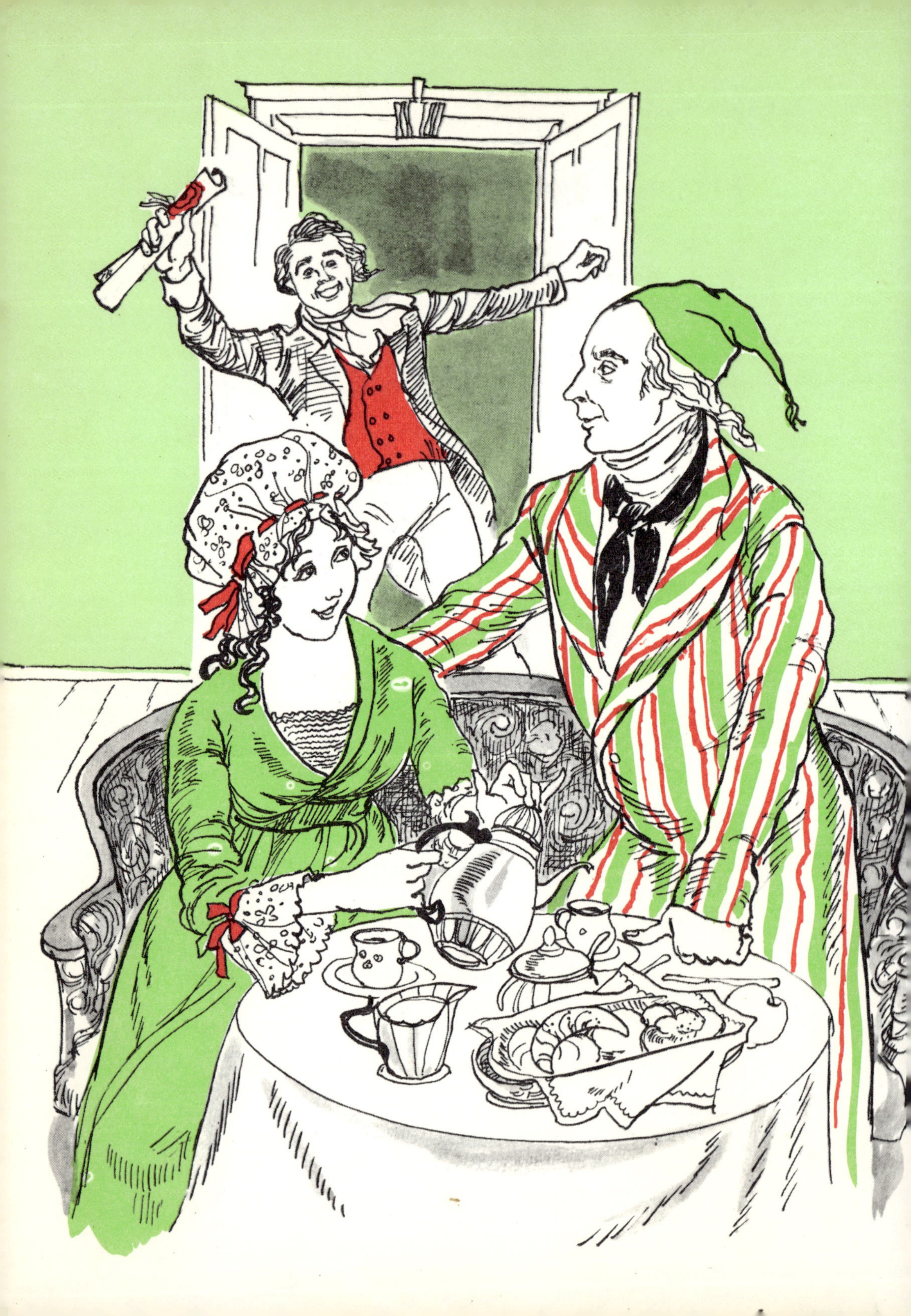

The Madisons moved to Washington, which was now the nation's capital. Dolly had many visitors. Jefferson noticed how well Dolly entertained. Jefferson's own wife had died, and his two daughters were both married. So he asked Dolly to be the nation's official hostess. Dolly did this charmingly.

During Jefferson's administration, the spirit of adventure and progress swept the nation. The United States bought the Louisiana Territory from France. Madison had worked hard for this.

The news reached Washington early on the morning of July 3, 1803.

Madison was awakened by the ringing of bells and the roaring of cannons.

A messenger burst in, shouting, "The United States has bought Louisiana!"

Madison hurried to the President's House to help prepare a statement. The next day there was a big celebration. Dolly rounded up her many helpers. Together they prepared cakes and drinks. These were served to hundreds of hungry people who crowded the streets. Everyone was excited.

The same eager spirit of progress was shown in an expedition to the Northwest. This was led by Captain Meriwether Lewis, Jefferson's secretary, and his friend, Captain William Clark. For years Jefferson had wanted to map the territory between the Mississippi River and the Pacific Ocean. Now, after careful preparation, Lewis and Clark set out. Before the men left, Dolly gave a big dinner in their honor.

A great tragedy occurred the following year. The Vice-President of the United States killed one of the nation's greatest statesmen—Aaron Burr shot Alexander Hamilton in a duel. Burr had been angered by something Hamilton had said about him. Everyone was shocked. Hamilton had been the nation's first Secretary of the Treasury. Dolly must have been horrified, because Burr had been her friend.

There was happiness for Dolly, however, as well as sadness. Dolly's sister, Anna, had recently married Richard Cutts. He was a congressman from Massachusetts. Because their husbands were both in the government, the two sisters still saw each other often.

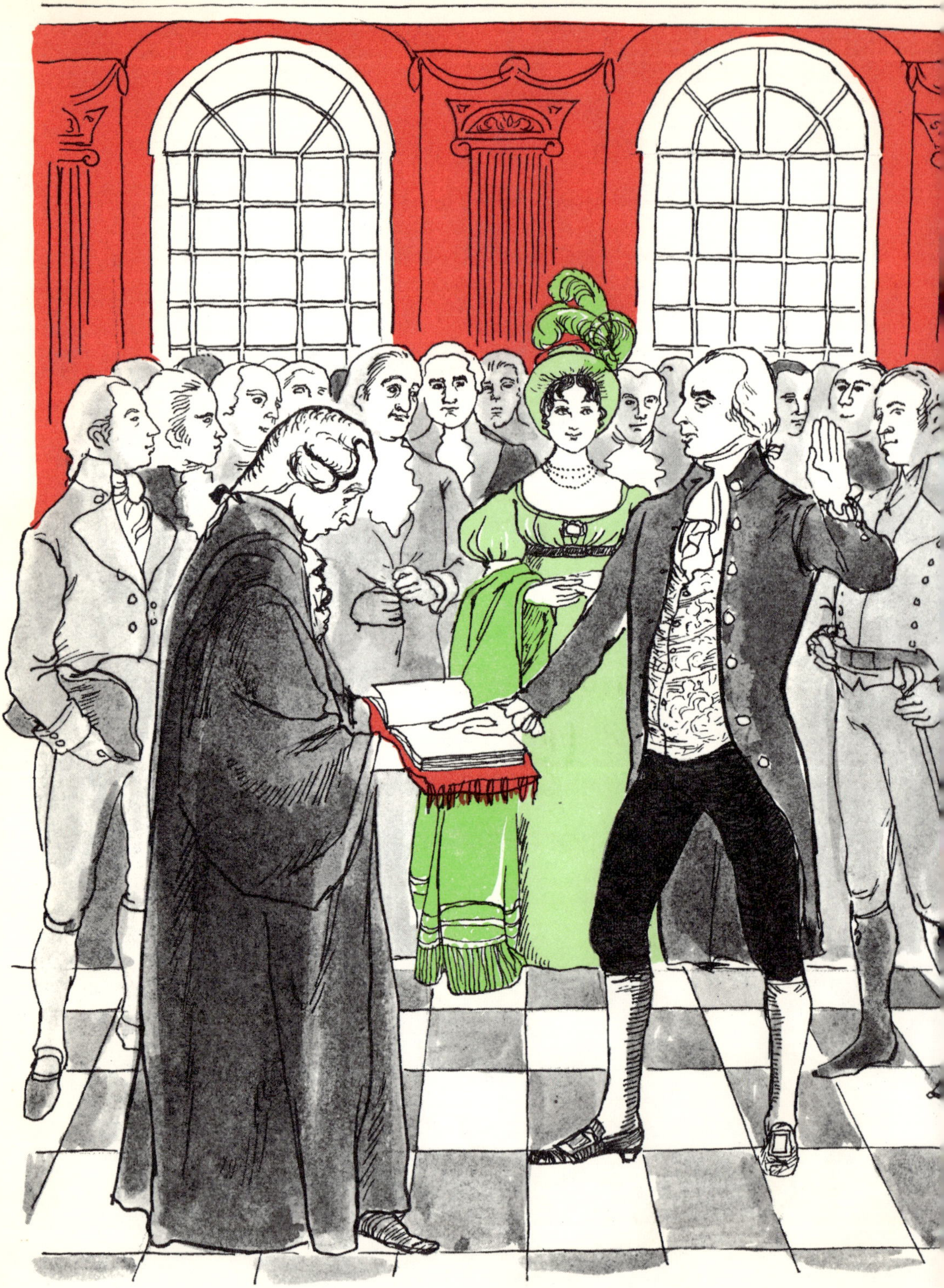

Chapter 7

The First Lady

In 1809 James Madison was inaugurated President of the United States. Dolly Madison was the new First Lady of the land.

Jefferson was glad to have his friend take his place. Dolly continued to act as official hostess.

Inauguration Day began with a long parade in honor of Madison. That night there was a gay Inaugural Ball.

This was the first Inaugural Ball in our history. It took place in a large hall in a hotel. The room was so crowded that windows had to be broken to let in enough air. Dolly was lovely in a yellow velvet dress. There were pearls at her neck and wrists. On her head was a turban from Paris with two beautiful plumes.

At first the Madisons had to live in their own home. Jefferson had brought his furniture and belongings to the empty President's House. Now he carted all his things back to his home, Monticello, in Virginia.

"I believe the President's House belongs to the people," Dolly said. "It should be beautiful and have things of its own."

Congress agreed and gave money for furniture. Dolly and an architect started picking things out.

Dolly decided to use many mirrors. "These will make the rooms seem larger and reflect the lights of the crystal chandeliers."

She had chairs, sofas, and hangings of yellow satin damask. Stuart's famous painting of George Washington was hung in the dining room. Dolly bought a piano, a guitar, and a parrot.

Dolly was now so popular that people copied everything she did. They copied her clothes. They copied her dinners. They copied what she said. Dolly was so interested in all people that she remembered not only the faces but also the names of everyone she met.

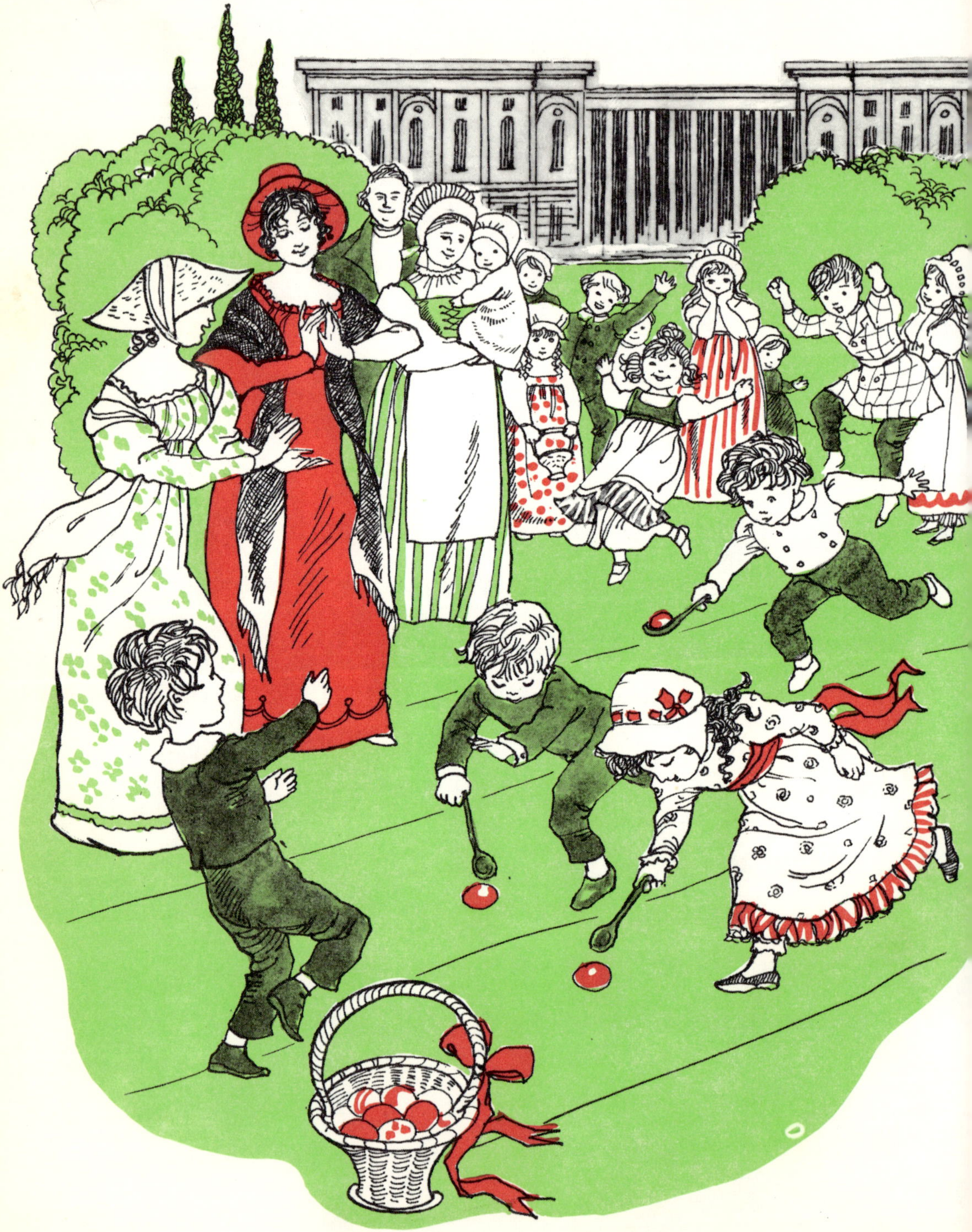

Dolly's dinners were famous. The table was piled with delicious foods of all kinds. Her ice cream, which was new then, proved to be very popular.

Dolly and Madison had no children other than Payne. But Dolly tried to make other people's children happy. She started Easter egg rolling on the front lawn of the Capitol building. She also helped to start an orphanage. She herself made clothes for the orphans.

Dolly's son, Payne, was a young man now. Dolly gave parties for his friends. She took them to the races. She sent Payne abroad. He never wrote home. He borrowed money from Madison but never returned it. Dolly could not stop loving Payne. But he made her very unhappy.

Chapter 8

Washington Burns

Ever since the Revolutionary War, America had had trouble with England. In 1812 war began again. At first the fighting was at sea and on the Great Lakes. Then in 1814, the British landed at the mouth of the Potomac River. They were marching to Washington, bent on burning the city.

Madison told Dolly, "My place, as Commander-in-Chief, is with the army. Would you be afraid to stay here with a guard?"

"No," said Dolly, firmly.

"Good. Save everything you can, especially my government papers. Pack them in trunks and send them to a safe place. I'll send word where I can meet you. Take care of yourself."

Soon after Madison left, Dolly went up to the housetop. Through her spy-glass she could faintly make out a moving line of men. She could hear the roar of distant cannons.

"John," she called to her faithful servant. "Come and help me pack Mr. Madison's papers."

The sound of cannons came nearer. Someone shouted, "The guard has fled!" But Dolly kept on working. She packed the silver and other valuables in big baskets ready to take away with her.

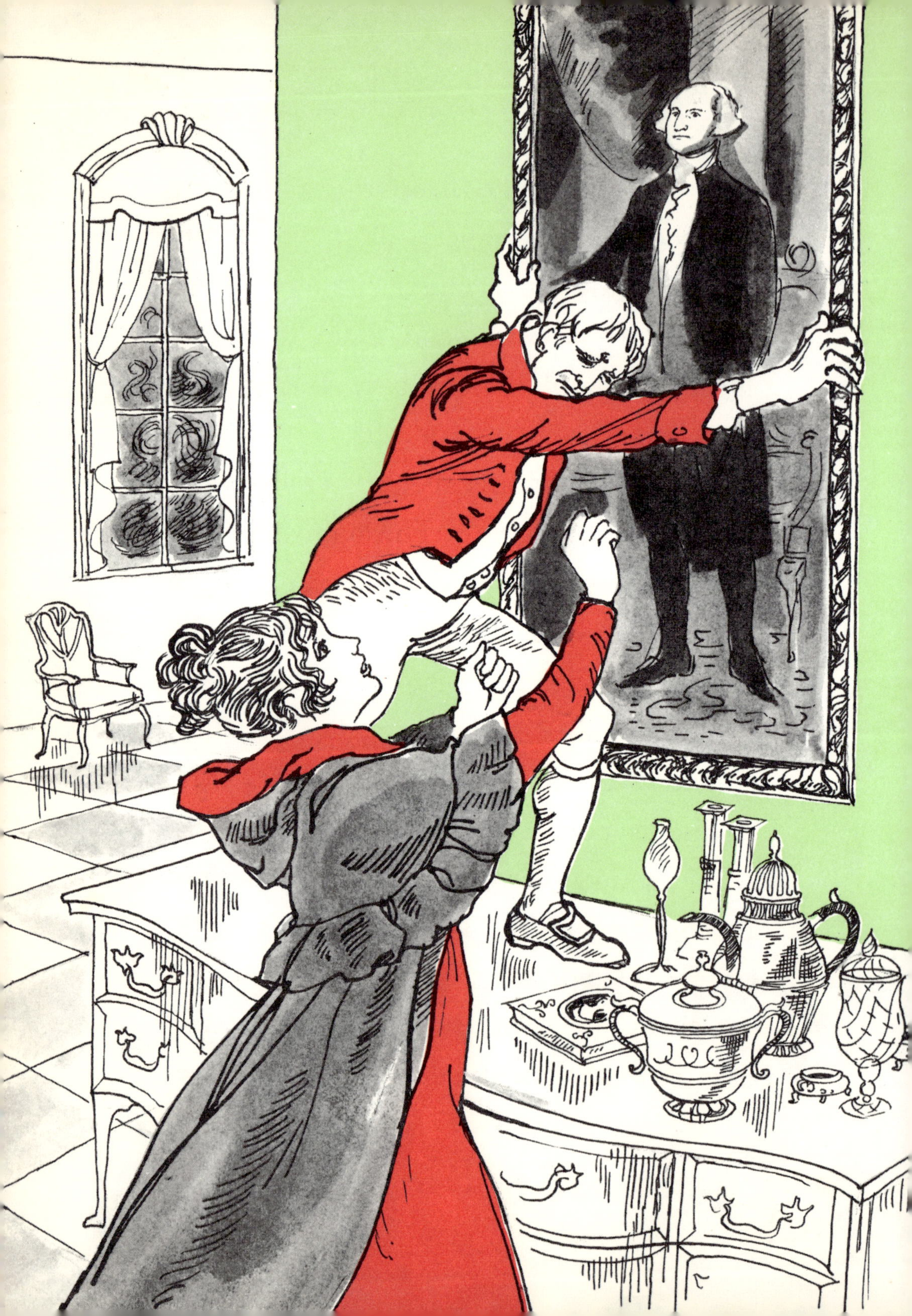

The next morning Dolly was calmly writing to her sister when a soldier dashed up. He brought a note from Madison.

"Leave at once," it said. "You are no longer safe."

Dolly started to leave. Then she thought of Stuart's portrait of Washington.

"We must save the painting of President Washington!" she called.

John found the frame was nailed to the wall.

"Break the frame," commanded Dolly.

John broke the frame. The picture was given to two men who carried it safely to New York.

Then Dolly and Sukey hurried away in a carriage. They took the silver and other valuables with them.

Roads out of the city were jammed with carts and people trying to escape.

The British came up steadily. They entered Washington. Shouting wildly, they set fire to the Capitol building. Then they burned down the Library of Congress with all its valuable books.

Next, they went to the President's House. Hundreds of soldiers roamed through the rooms. They piled Dolly's beautiful furniture and Madison's books in the center of the rooms. They threw balls of fire through the windows. Soon the flames leaped up. The heat was so great, it melted some statues and glass chandeliers.

Meanwhile, Dolly and Sukey dashed through Georgetown at top speed. They spent the first night at a soldiers' camp.

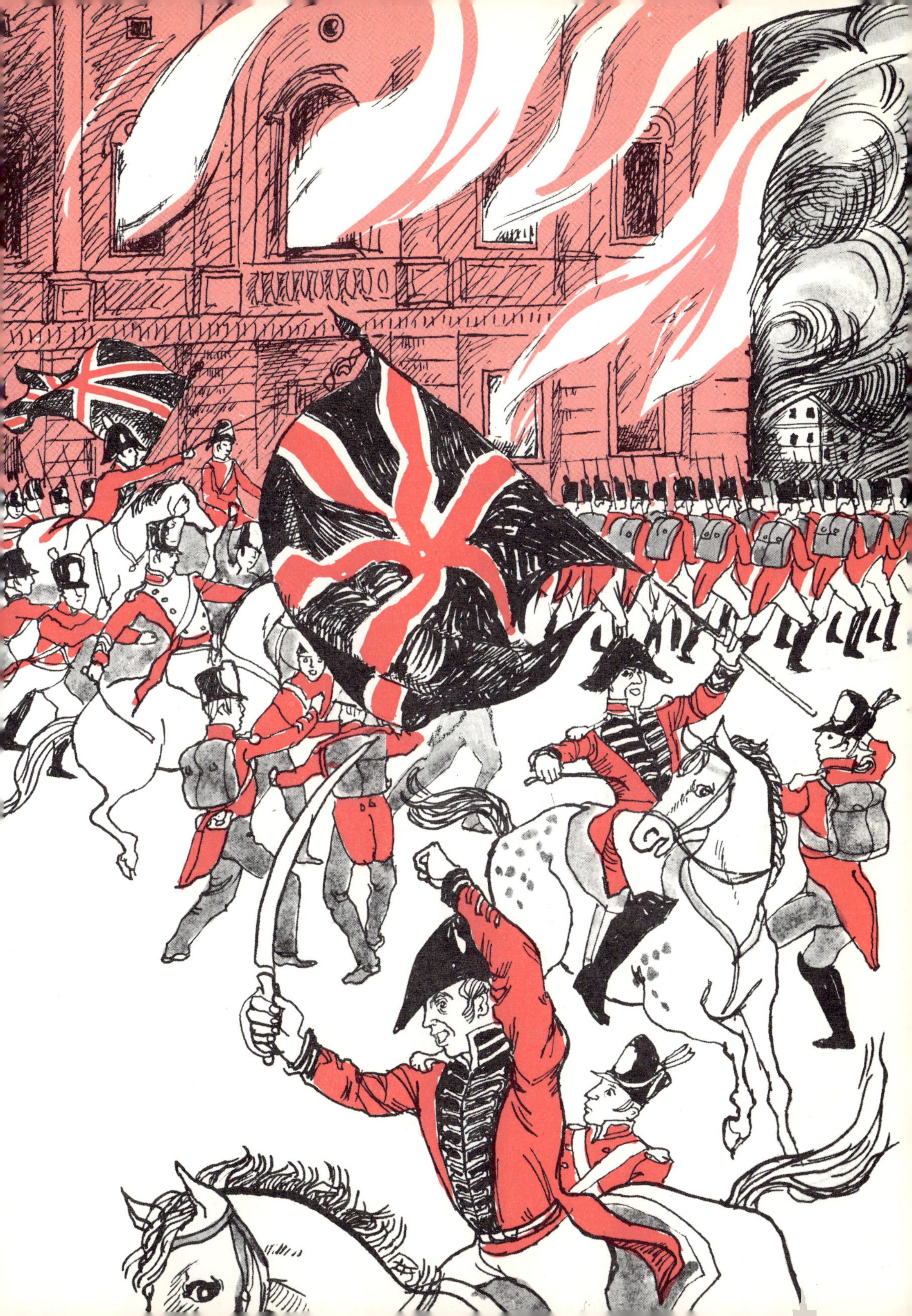

The next day Dolly drove to the place where she had arranged to meet Madison. He was there, and they talked. But a report came that he was in danger. So he and his guards fled into the woods for safety.

Now Dolly was on her own. She sent Sukey away in the carriage with the silver. Then she dressed like a poor country woman and started off in a farm wagon. Two men went with her.

For two days Dolly drove through the country. People feared she was lost.

Meanwhile, a terrible hurricane hit Washington. It ripped the roofs off houses and tipped over the British cannons. For hours the rain fell in torrents, putting out the fires. The British became tired and discouraged.

They were happy when orders came to leave the ruined city.

Dolly found her way to the Potomac River. The bridge to Washington was down at both ends. Dolly saw an officer in a ferry boat. She asked him to take her across. He looked at her ragged clothes and refused.

"I am the President's wife," she said.

The officer laughed, "You really don't expect me to believe that!"

Finally she convinced him. He took her across the river to Washington. She found only rubble and ashes where great buildings had stood.

Dolly drove at once to her sister, Anna Cutts. Anna's house was still standing. Here Madison joined Dolly. At last they were together and safe.

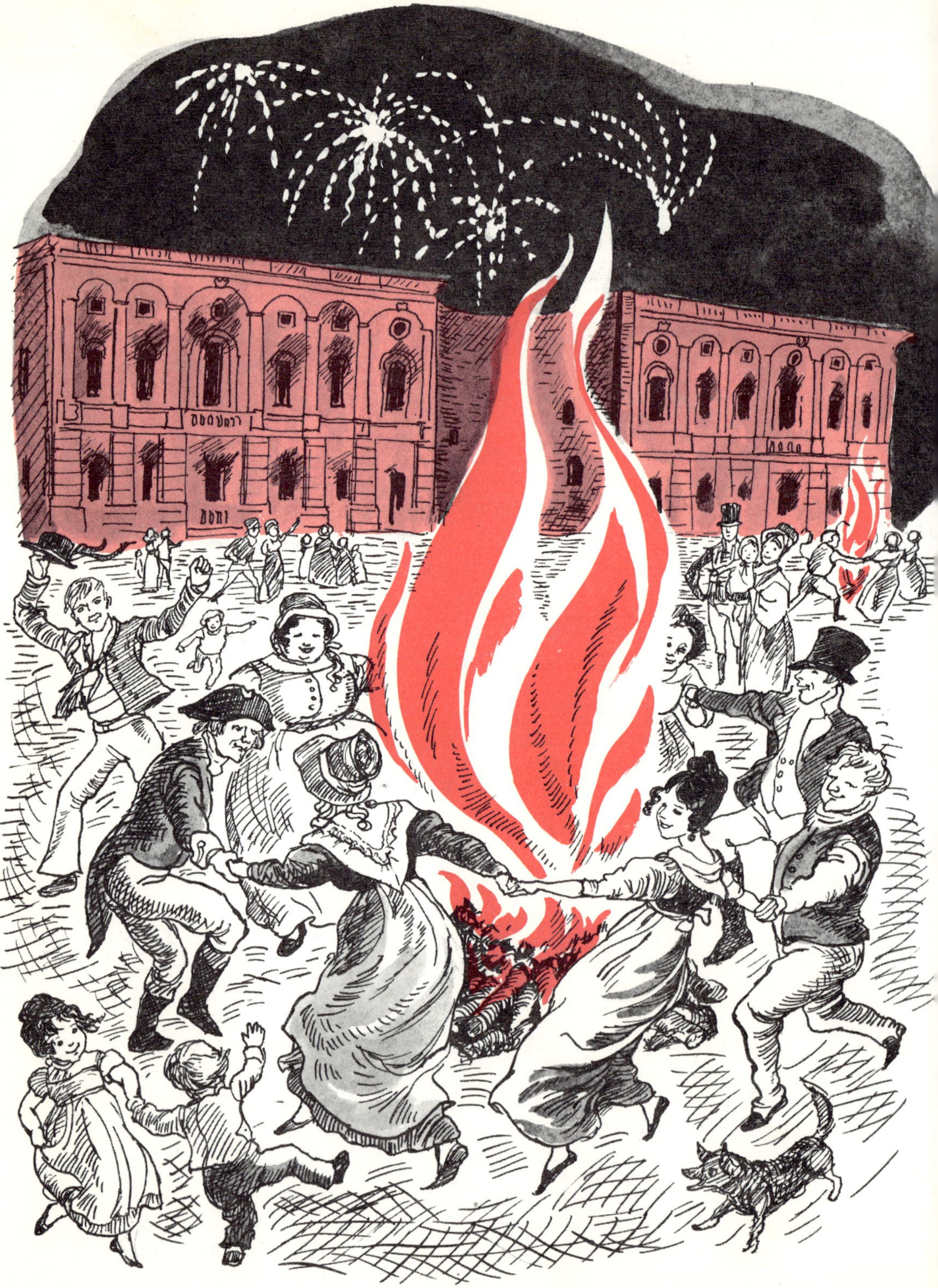

Chapter 9

Rebuilding the Capital

General Andrew Jackson won a great victory over the British at New Orleans in 1815. Very soon afterwards came wonderful news. A treaty had been signed with England. The people went wild. Bells rang. Fireworks lighted the sky. Bonfires blazed from Boston to Washington.

The Madisons were living in Octagon House. Crowds of people filled the drawing room. Dolly, happy and relaxed, looked her loveliest.

Now, the first job was to rebuild Washington. The architect Benjamin Henry Latrobe was called in. He had helped plan the capital earlier. Now he cut down trees along Pennsylvania Avenue to make room for new buildings.

The Capitol itself consisted of two great buildings with a muddy walk between. Charles Bulfinch of Boston put in a central building, connecting the two already there. Bulfinch planned a dome to go above the central part.

The Library of Congress with all its priceless books was gone. In order to start the new Library, Thomas Jefferson sent his own books. There were several thousand of them. Ten yoke of oxen pulled the precious books from Monticello to Washington.

The inside of the President's House was entirely burned out. But the outer walls remained. These, black with smoke, were now painted white. The Madisons lived in a house on Pennsylvania Avenue while this work was being done. When the work was finished, they moved back into the President's House.

Because it was painted white, the President's House was soon being called the White House. This name has lasted through the years.

Dolly still gave her delightful parties. She still found time to help the orphans. And every day boys and girls gathered outside the window where her famous parrot sat in the sunshine.

By the end of his second term, Madison was 66 years old. He had been President of the United States for eight years. He had led the nation through a war. He had seen Washington burned to the ground, then rebuilt through his tireless efforts. He had been unpopular at first because many people disliked the idea of war. But he was much loved by the end of his Presidency.

Now Madison was ready to retire from politics. Dolly, although seventeen years younger, was also tired of political life. They were both glad to leave the Presidency to their good friend James Monroe. They longed to go home to beautiful Montpelier.

Chapter 10

Montpelier

Montpelier was larger than ever. It covered between three and four thousand acres. There were fields of tobacco and grain, and meadows for the grazing cattle. The house itself was large, and the rooms were bright and airy.

Madison's father had died. But Madison's mother still lived in her wing of the house. She and Dolly became close friends. Dolly took all her famous guests to call on the old lady.

The most important room in the house was the library. But it was so jammed with books and papers that Madison worked in his sitting room. He was completing his record of the Constitutional Convention. Dolly helped him copy his papers.

Many guests came to Montpelier. Dolly never knew how many would be there for meals, or to spend the night. One day there were 90 people at an outdoor dinner. But there was plenty of food, and room to spare.

One very important guest was General Lafayette. He was the famous French general who had helped America win the Revolutionary War.

Lafayette landed in New York where he received a great public welcome. He visited Jefferson, who was now an old man. Then Lafayette with his son, friends, secretary, and servants came to Montpelier.

"They're coming! They're coming!" called a little boy.

Up the long drive, wound a long procession of coaches and men on horse-back. They drew near the house. There on the porch, the Madison family was gathered.

"Welcome, General!" they all shouted. "Welcome!"

Lafayette stayed several weeks with the Madisons. He was interested in Dolly's garden. Later he sent her lilies from France. He sat with Madison by the fire. They talked about the affairs of the United States and France.

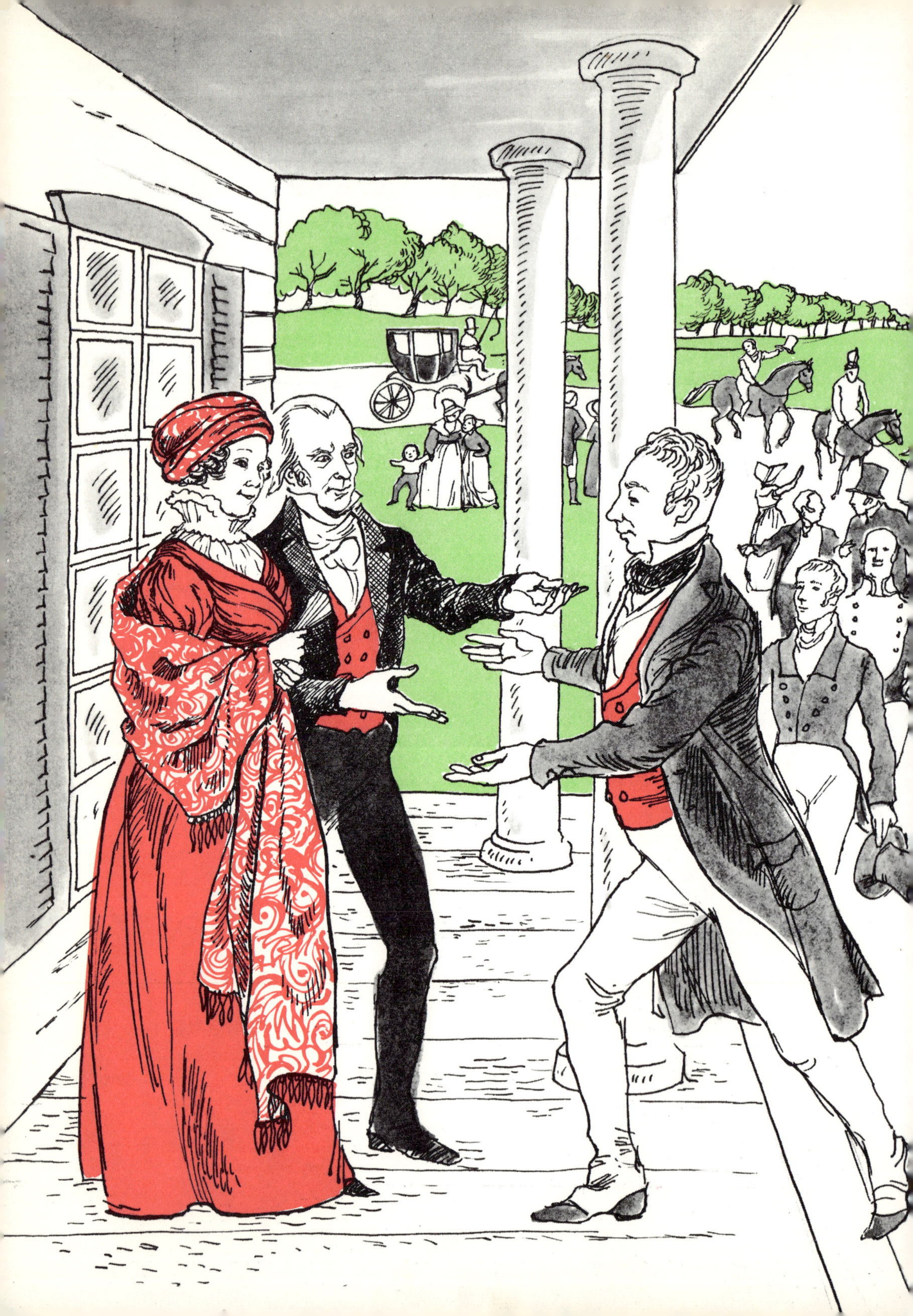

All this entertaining was delightful, but expensive. Madison had to sell some of his land to pay his bills. But guests kept coming.

Meanwhile Payne was in Europe, having a gay time. He sent home for so much money that Madison had to cut off his allowance. Then no word came for months. Finally, they learned that Payne was in prison for not paying his debts. Money was sent at once, and Payne came home.

The years passed. Each year found Dolly a little older, a little more tired. Each year Madison suffered more and more from rheumatism. After a while he had to be taken around in a wheel-chair. But he was always cheerful, never complaining.

Dolly never left his side. For twenty years this gay, lively woman stayed at Montpelier. She used all her ability and charm to keep her beloved husband happy.

Suddenly Madison grew much weaker. On June 28, 1836, he died. He had been so quiet and brave that no one realized how weak he really was.

With Madison's death the nation lost one of its most devoted and brilliant statesmen. His ability and his hard work at the Constitutional Convention won him the name "Father of the Constitution."

Chapter 11

Dolly's Last Years

In his will Madison left Montpelier to Dolly. She decided to put her son in charge of the farm. Dolly hoped he would really get to work at last. She left Payne alone and returned to Washington. She was now sixty-nine.

Dolly owned a small house in the center of the city. Anna Payne, her brother's daughter, lived there with her.

Soon Dolly was entertaining again. Her old friends came to see her often.

She gave several parties. One was a gay wedding reception when her nephew, Richard Cutts, married the granddaughter of Thomas Jefferson.

Usually, at these parties, Dolly wore the same black velvet gown. She had only little money now, and her other dresses were shabby. But her charm and dignity had not changed.

Payne at Montpelier kept his mother poor. Because he had never worked, he did not know how.

To help him, Dolly mortgaged her Washington house. Finally she had to sell beautiful Montpelier with its gardens and great trees. She kept only the family burial ground and a little furniture. Later she sold her valuable Stuart paintings and some silver.

Sometimes Dolly would have gone hungry had it not been for the Daniel Websters. They lived across the street from her and sent her food.

On Dolly's eightieth birthday a wonderful thing happened. Congress bought her husband's records of the Constitutional Convention for $25,000. Dolly had been trying to sell the papers for years. They were put in the Library of Congress. They are still kept there.

The money came at the time of Dolly's greatest need. It changed everything. Her fear of poverty was gone.

Congress gave Dolly a seat in the House of Representatives. From here, she could watch everything going on. Never before had a seat in the House been given to any woman.

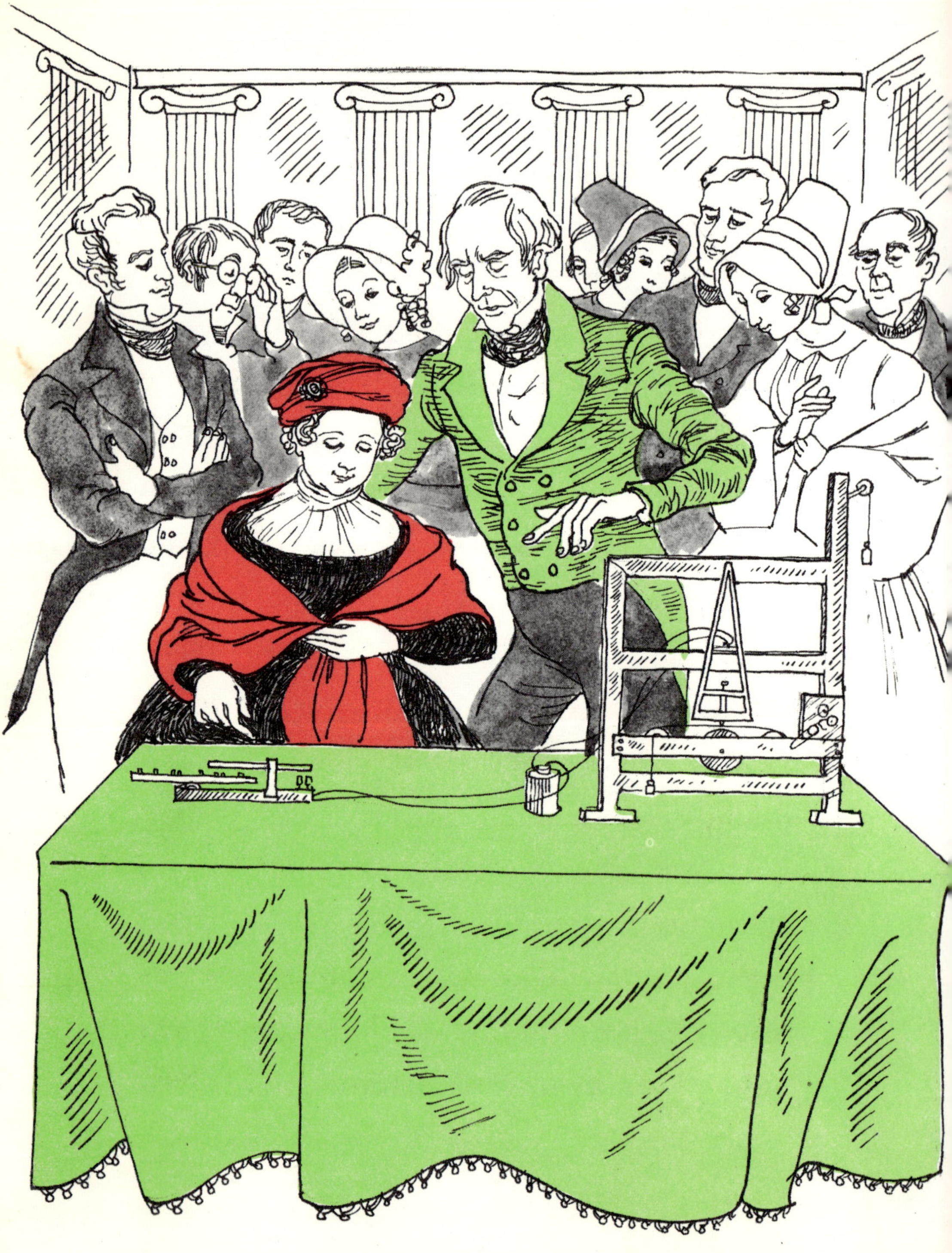

Dolly was an old lady now. But she was still invited to every big public event. Samuel F. B. Morse, the inventor, asked her to be one of a small group present when his first telegram was sent. It was sent from near Baltimore to Washington.

"What hath God wrought" was the message that came over the telegraph wire.

Mr. Morse turned to Dolly. "Mrs. Madison, would you send a return message?"

Dolly thought a moment. Then she sent greetings to an old friend in Baltimore.

Dolly was also present when the corner-stone of the Washington Monument was laid. She, who had known and loved

Washington, rode in the parade to honor him.

Dolly's last public appearance was at President Polk's farewell ball. The White House was brilliantly lighted and crowded with people. Toward the end of the ball, the President asked Dolly to walk about with him. Dolly was dressed in a white satin gown and white satin turban. Slowly she went through the rooms on the President's arm. The people all greeted her with deep affection.

The summer of 1849 was very hot. Dolly did not complain, but she felt ill. She went to bed and was content to stay there. One night she fell quietly asleep. In the morning she did not awaken.

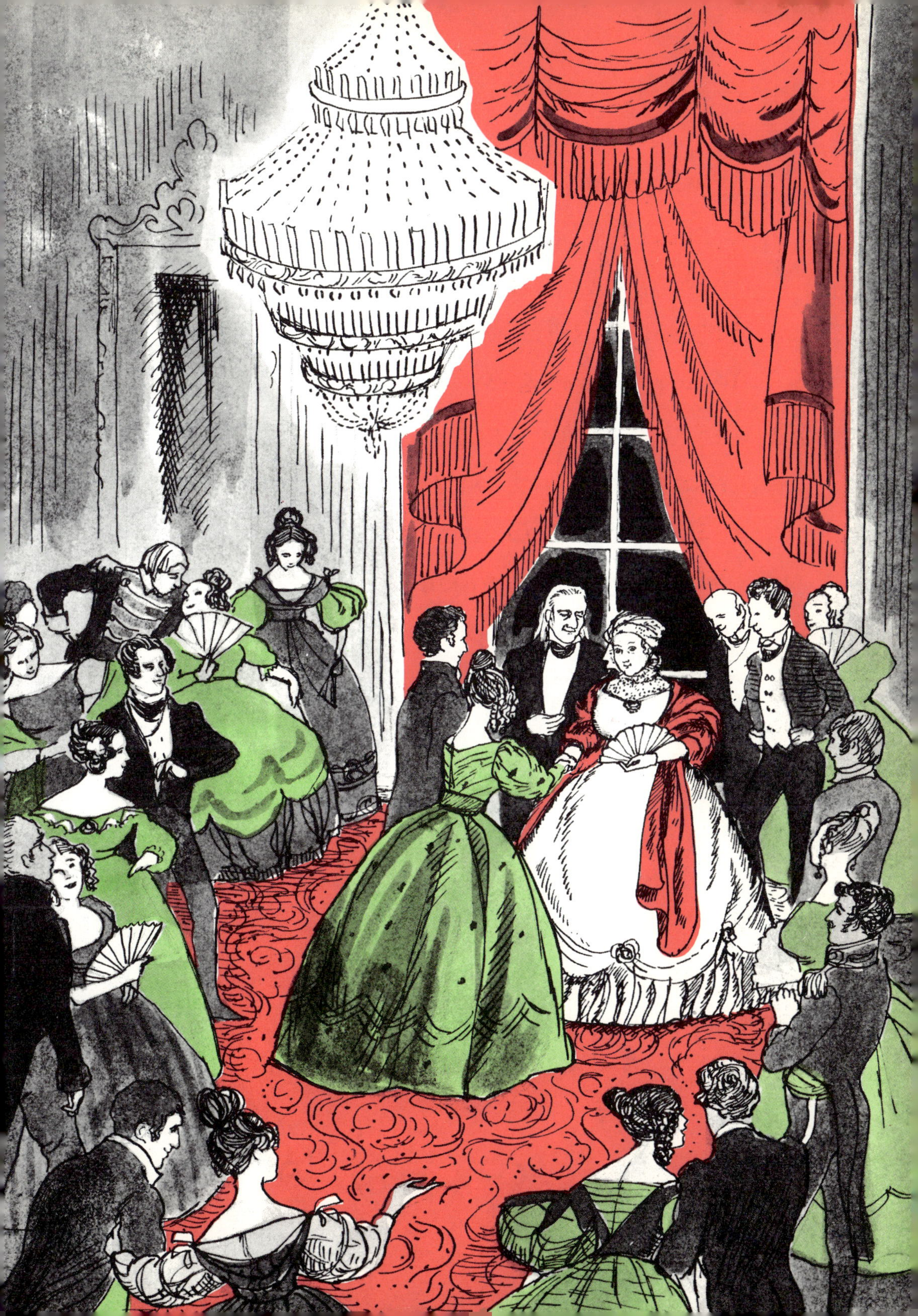

All Washington turned out at Dolly's funeral. The President and members of the Cabinet were there. The Senate and House of Representatives marched in the funeral procession. There were officers of the army and navy, ambassadors from foreign countries, and members of the Supreme Court.

Dolly had touched the lives of thousands of people and had left them all happier for having known her. The secret of her popularity may be found in her conversation with a visiting Frenchman.

"Everyone loves Mrs. Madison," he said smiling down at her.

Dolly answered quickly, "Mrs. Madison loves everybody."